Note to parents, carers and teachers

Read it yourself is a series of modern stories, favourite characters and traditional tales written in a simple way for children who are learning to read. The books can be read independently or as part of a guided reading session.

Each book is carefully structured to include many high-frequency words vital for first reading. The sentences on each page are supported closely by pictures to help with understanding, and to offer lively details to talk about.

The books are graded into four levels that progressively introduce wider vocabulary and longer stories as a reader's ability and confidence grows.

Ideas for use

- Begin by looking through the book and talking about the pictures. Has your child heard this story before?
- Help your child with any words he does not know, either by helping him to sound them out or supplying them yourself.
- Developing readers can be concentrating so hard on the words that they sometimes don't fully grasp the meaning of what they're reading. Answering the puzzle questions on pages 30 and 31 will help with understanding.

For more information and advice on Read it yourself and book banding, visit **www.ladybird.com/readityourself**

Book Band 4

Level 1 is ideal for children who have received some initial reading instruction. Each story is told very simply, using a small number of frequently repeated words.

Special features:

Opening pages introduce key story words

Large, clear type

Careful match between story and pictures

Educational Consultant: Geraldine Taylor
Book Banding Consultant: Kate Ruttle

A catalogue record for this book is available from the British Library

Published by Ladybird Books Ltd
80 Strand, London, WC2R 0RL
A Penguin Company

002

ISBN: 978-0-72327-263-2

Printed in China

The Ugly Duckling

Illustrated by Richard Johnson

Mother Duck

The eggs

The Ugly Duckling
The ducklings

Once upon a time,
there were seven eggs.

Six ducklings
were beautiful.
One duckling was not.

"You are ugly,"
said Mother Duck.

"Go away."

The Ugly Duckling
met a cow.

"You are ugly,"
said the cow.
"Go away."

The Ugly Duckling
met a cat.

"You are ugly,"
said the cat.
"Go away."

The Ugly Duckling
met a rabbit.

"You are ugly,"
said the rabbit.
"Go away."

The Ugly Duckling
met a boy.

"You are ugly,"
said the boy.
"Go away."

The Ugly Duckling
met a girl.

"You are ugly,"
said the girl.
"Go away."

The Ugly Duckling
was all alone.

He was very sad.

One day, the Ugly Duckling saw some beautiful swans.

"Look in the water," said the swans.

“You are beautiful,”
said the swans.
“Come with us.”

And he did.

How much do you remember about the story of The Ugly Duckling? Answer these questions and find out!

- How many eggs are there in the nest?
- What does everyone tell the Ugly Duckling to do?
- What does the Ugly Duckling see when he looks in the water?

Look at the pictures from the story and say the order they should go in.

A

B

C

D

Answer: C, D, B, A.

Read it yourself with Ladybird

Tick the books you've read!

Level 1

For children who are ready to take their first steps in reading.

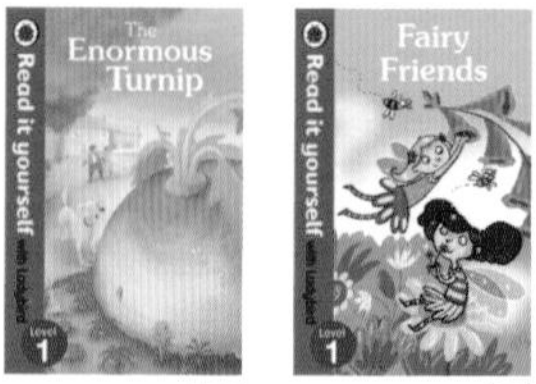

Level 2

For beginner readers who can read short, simple sentences with help.